The Ma

by Kevin Kramer   illustrated by Rusty Fletcher

Orlando   Boston   Dallas   Chicago   San Diego

Visit *The Learning Site!*

www.harcourtschool.com

Printed in China

ISBN 0-15-325410-6

11 12 13 14 15 16 17 18 19 20   121 10 09 08 07 06 05

Ordering Options
ISBN 0-15-323766-X (Collection)
ISBN 0-15-329526-0 (package of 5)

The mouse sat.

 The snake sat.

The cat sat.

 The monkey sat.

The hippo sat.

 The elephant sat.

The mouse sat.